Big Teeth, No Teeth

Written by Ratu Mataira

Rigby

big teeth

Look at the lion.
It has big teeth.

lizard

no teeth

Look at this lizard.
Where are the teeth?

This lizard has no teeth. 3

big teeth

Look at the tiger.
It has big teeth.

4

snail

no teeth

Look at the snail.
Where are the teeth?

The snail has no teeth.

5

Look!
The crocodile has
big teeth.
It has a big mouth, too.

teeth

mouth

The frog has a
big mouth, too.

It has no teeth.

mouth

horse

teeth

Look at the horse and the hippo.

hippo

teeth

They have big teeth.

11

shark

whale

Look at the shark
and the whale.
They have big teeth.

turtle

Look at the turtle.
Where are the teeth?

The turtle has no teeth.

Look at the animals.

Big teeth

No teeth

Index

big teeth
    crocodile. 6
    hippo. 10
    horse 10
    lion. 2
    shark 12
    tiger. 4
    whale. 12
no teeth
    frog 8
    lizard 3
    snail. 5
    turtle 13

Guide Notes

Title: Big Teeth, No Teeth
Stage: Early (1) – Red

Genre: Nonfiction
Approach: Guided Reading
Processes: Thinking Critically, Exploring Language, Processing Information
Written and Visual Focus: Photographs (static images), Index, Labels
Word Count: 100

THINKING CRITICALLY
(sample questions)
- Tell the children this book is about some animals that have big teeth and some animals that have no teeth.
- Look at the title and read it to the children.
- Ask them what animals they know of that have big teeth or no teeth.
- Focus the children's attention on the index. Ask: "What are you going to find out about in this book?"
- If you want to find out about a crocodile with big teeth, which page would you look on?
- If you want to find out about a lion with big teeth, which page would you look on?
- Why do you think some animals have teeth?
- How do you think some animals might eat with no teeth?
- What do you think might be different about the food that animals with teeth and no teeth eat?

EXPLORING LANGUAGE

Terminology
Title, cover, photographs, author, photographers

Vocabulary
Interest words: teeth, tiger, lizard, mouth, snail, crocodile, frog, shark, turtle, horse
High-frequency words: it, where, have

Print Conventions
Capital letter for sentence beginnings, periods, commas, exclamation mark, question marks